Jake
and the
Babysitter

Jake's bear

This Jake book

belongs to . .

. . . .

also by Simon James
The Day Jake Vacuumed

To Clare and Daniel and our adventures – with love

First published 1991 by Simon James

This Picturemac edition published 1993
by Pan Macmillan Children's Books
a division of Pan Macmillan Publishers Limited
Cavaye Place London SW10 9PG
and Basingstoke

Associated companies throughout the world

ISBN 0-333-58335-3

9 8 7 6 5 4 3 2

A CIP catalogue record for this book is available from
the British Library

Printed in Hong Kong

Jake

and the
Babysitter

Simon James

M

PAN MACMILLAN CHILDREN'S BOOKS

It was the night the babysitter was coming and Jake was in a mood. Of course no one who knew Jake would babysit for him. So his father had phoned the new neighbour.

Jake's
secret stolen
bisket box

Jake's parents were worried.
His mother sighed. "Perhaps he's changed
his mind."
But at last there was a knock on the door.
"You must be our new neighbour," said
Jake's father. "It's so nice of you to come."

Upstairs Jake and Timmy prepared for battle.
Once his parents had left they sneaked down
to watch the late film.
But after a while the babysitter started making
strange sniffing noises, as if he could smell
someone in the room …

Suddenly a huge hairy hand pulled Jake out
from under the settee.
This certainly wasn't the new neighbour.
It was the most enormous babysitter
Jake had ever seen.
Jake tried to smile

and the babysitter smiled back.
For a moment Jake thought the
babysitter might eat him, so he
quickly pointed to the kitchen.

The babysitter, Timmy and Jake crept past
his sister's bedroom. Then they bounced up
and down on Jake's bed – until the legs broke.

They slid back down the banisters to the lounge,

where they danced to old Elvis Parsley
records that belonged to Jake's dad.
Finally, they sat down to watch a really scary
horror film.

It was nearly midnight and time for Jake's parents to come home. How could Jake explain what had happened to the house?

Perhaps it was time for bed, he thought.

When Jake's parents got home they couldn't
believe their eyes. How could the babysitter
have made such a terrible mess?
They refused to pay him and ordered him to
leave immediately.
But the babysitter didn't really care ...

And the next day neither did Jake.
He knew he'd had the best babysitter – ever!

love from the
Babysitter